# Shivers

## TERROR ON TROLL MOUNTAIN

### M. D. Spenser

Paradise Press, Inc.

**Plantation, Florida**

To M.B. without whom this book would not have been written

Published by Paradise Press, Inc. by arrangement with River Publishing, Inc. All right, title and interest to the "SHIVERS" logo and design are owned by River Publishing, Inc. No portion of the "SHIVERS" logo and design may be reproduced in part or whole without prior written permission from River Publishing, Inc. An application for a registered trademark of the "SHIVERS" logo and design is pending with the Federal Patent and Trademark office.

ISBN 1-57657-050-9

EXCLUSIVE DISTRIBUTION BY PARADISE PRESS, INC.

Cover Design by George Paturzo
Cover Illustration by Eddie Roseboom

Printed in the U.S.A.
30571

# Chapter One

Paul Alberti was *supposed* to be seeing the snow-capped mountains of Northern Italy, for the first time in his life.

Instead, he sat stuffed in the tiny back seat of his Uncle Freddy's car, staring at his beat-up red sneakers — and trying very hard not to lose his lunch.

"Come on, Paul!" called Mr. Alberti from the front seat. "You can stare at your sneakers back in Chicago. Look out the window. You're missing the best view!"

Paul's father knew all the best views. He had grown up in these mountains before he moved to the United States as a young man.

"Can't," Paul moaned.

He was trying to move as little as possible. And trying to speak as slowly as possible, too. Anything to avoid unnecessary motion.

1

"Still . . . car . . . sick," he croaked.

Mr. Alberti laughed loudly.

He had a thick mustache and an even thicker Italian accent. He loved to laugh and crack jokes — which sometimes embarrassed Paul, only because his dad was so *loud*.

"Maybe you should've stopped after just two sandwiches at the airport!" Mr. Alberti boomed, and laughed again. One of his favorite things to joke about was Paul's humongous appetite.

He laughed so loudly that Uncle Freddy started chuckling, too, even though he couldn't possibly understand what they were talking about.

Uncle Freddy was Mr. Alberti's younger brother. He still lived in Italy. The only English words Uncle Freddy knew were "cool" and "bye-bye."

After they finally stopped laughing, Mr. Alberti turned around in the front passenger seat to look at Paul.

"Don't worry, buddy," he said. "We're almost there."

"There" — the place they were headed — was Pinzolo, which is pronounced PEEN-so-low. Pinzolo was the mountain village where Paul's dad grew up, and where Uncle Freddy still lived.

Paul had just turned twelve years old, and Mr. Alberti had decided he was old enough to appreciate a three-week visit to Italy. Paul's mom couldn't come because she was a ballet dancer and would be touring all summer.

Paul was pretty tall for a twelve year old, almost as tall as his dad — who was actually pretty short for a forty-five year old. Some people thought Paul could stand to lose a few pounds, but he didn't agree. He just enjoyed food, that was all.

He had dark brown hair and wore thick, clunky glasses, which made him look like a nerd. But he wasn't, really.

The two most striking things about Paul, everyone agreed, were his feet. They were *huge.* Even though he was tall, they didn't fit his body quite right.

To put it bluntly, they were clodhoppers. If footballs were the size of Paul's feet, it would take a whole team to catch one. If Paul was on a sinking ship, a family of four could use one of his shoes for a raft.

Those were the kinds of jokes Paul had to put up with at school. Every day.

Now, he sat trapped in a tiny car, forced to stare at the same feet that gave him so much trouble. All so he wouldn't throw up all over the back seat of his Uncle Freddy's car.

Normally, Paul didn't get car sick. But he'd just spent eight long hours on a crowded, noisy airplane, flying all the way from Chicago to Milan, one of the bigger cities in Northern Italy. Now he had to ride three hours in a car from Milan to Pinzolo.

Uncle Freddy had picked them up at the airport.

Uncle Freddy's real name was Federico, which sort of translates to "Frederick." He was shorter than Paul's dad, and almost bald. A few wisps of hair made a messy ring around his head. Uncle Freddy was the type of guy who didn't believe in combs.

He was a great uncle. But he wasn't exactly the greatest *driver* in the world. He liked to shift gears a lot, so the car always lurched back and forth. He also liked to drive fast, even on windy mountain roads, which upset Paul's stomach even more.

Plus, it was a hot summer day. Cars in Italy use diesel gasoline, which smells really bad and gave Paul a headache.

OK, all right, Paul thought. Maybe he *shouldn't* have eaten that third sandwich at the airport. He just enjoyed food, that was all.

For all of those reasons, Paul was looking green at the moment.

His mom always told him, "If you ever feel carsick, stare straight ahead, right through the windshield, as far up the road as you can see. Then you'll be focused, and you won't feel as queasy."

The problem was that here, among the beautiful, snow-capped mountains of Northern Italy, the roads were so twisty and turny you couldn't stare more than ten feet in front of the car before another curve came along.

So Paul had fallen back on Plan B - staring at his shoes.

"How much longer till we get there?" he asked. His stomach was starting to feel better, but his neck was getting sore.

No one answered. Paul stared at his feet some

5

more.

"Did you hear me?" he asked.

Still, no one answered.

It felt like the car was going faster. Paul decided to risk it and look up.

The first thing he noticed was that Uncle Freddy wasn't smiling. Uncle Freddy *always* smiled.

Now he seemed almost . . . scared.

"What's the matter?" Paul asked his dad.

Mr. Alberti was talking to Uncle Freddy in Italian. Very quietly.

Another bad sign. When Paul's dad lowered his voice, it almost always meant trouble.

The car rocketed ahead even faster.

"Speak English!" Paul cried. "What's wrong? Why doesn't he slow down?"

They bore down on a curve in the road. Fast.

The car gained speed.

Uncle Freddy stomped on different pedals and moved the gear shift around. The car did not slow down.

"Why can't we stop?" Paul asked again.

He looked out his window and saw a steep

drop down the mountainside. A mountainside covered with sharp rocks and pointed trees.

Uncle Freddy shouted something in Italian. Paul didn't understand, but it didn't sound good.

Paul looked out the windshield again. They were barreling straight toward a flimsy wooden barrier that separated the road from the open space beyond.

"*Noooo!*" he shouted.

It was too late. The car crashed through the barrier at 90 miles per hour and went flying over the edge!

# Chapter Two

"Paul! Wake up, Paul! Wake up!"

It sounded to Paul as if his dad's voice was coming from the bottom of a deep well.

Slowly, he opened his eyes.

The first thing he realized was that he had been having a bad dream. He was OK. His dad was OK. The car was OK.

The second thing he realized was that he had fallen asleep in a very uncomfortable position on Uncle Freddy's back seat. One of his arms was twisted behind his head and his knees were pushed up practically to his chest. He felt like one giant cramp.

The third thing Paul realized — the best thing of all — was that the car had finally stopped moving.

They had arrived. They were in Pinzolo.

Mr. Alberti shook one of Paul's big feet.

"Are you all right, buddy?"

8

Paul nodded. He felt kind of groggy.

"Well come on, then. Everyone wants to see you. We're here."

Paul stretched his sore legs and climbed slowly out of the car. They had parked on a street lined with old, gray houses. It was a sunny afternoon. Paul blinked, still dazed from his nap.

Before he had time to take in much of the street, he was overwhelmed by a single sound. The sound of lots of voices. All shouting at the same time. All shouting the same thing.

"PAULO!" they shouted.

In Italian, Paul becomes "Paulo." They pronounced it POW (like a superhero punching a bad guy) and LOW (like the score you'd get on a quiz you didn't study for). POW-low.

At first, Paul was confused from having been asleep for so long. Who were these strange people? Why were they shouting this strange word?

Then he realized they were shouting at him.

Soon he was being hugged. And kissed. On both cheeks. Someone mussed his hair. Someone else squeezed his arm. A third person gave him a playful punch in the stomach that kind of hurt.

Everyone talked at once. Very loudly. He heard the word "grande" a lot. He knew that meant big. He assumed they were using the word to describe him. It sure wasn't being used to describe his father.

Eventually, he started matching up the names and faces in the crowd.

Paul had lots of relatives in Italy. He'd never met most of them. He'd seen photographs, of course, but people looked different in person.

Whoever they were, they were all very excited to meet Paulo.

The one person Paul *had* met before was his grandmother, Bianca. That's pronounced BEE-yan-KA, and it means "white" in Italian. Paul's grandmother was actually fairly pink, though, especially in her cheeks. She was short and round. Paul had to bend down to give her a hug.

She had been to Chicago several times to visit, and she hugged Paul longer than any of the others did.

Then there was Aunt Nat, Uncle Freddy's wife. Her real name in Italian was "Natalia," which translates to Natalie. Aunt Nat was tall and round. She was also a notorious cheek-pincher. She couldn't help herself. Every time she saw Paul, she reached over for a squeeze.

The rest of the crowd included cousins, friends of cousins, distant relatives and people who just happened to wander by.

Everyone had a great name. There was Carlo and Sergio, Pina and Nina, Maria Louisa Grazia and Pat. (Pat was short for something very complicated that Paul quickly forgot.)

After Paul's cheeks were red and sore from so many kisses and pinches, the party moved inside his grandmother's house. The house was big and roomy, and much, much older than most of the houses Paul had seen in Chicago.

Paul's grandmother, Bianca, yanked him into the kitchen. It seemed as if dozens of pots and pans were bubbling and steaming and sizzling all at once.

"You like?" she asked. She had learned some very basic English when she came to visit in Chicago.

Paul had no idea what was cooking, but it was food — and he liked food. Also, it smelled wonderful.

He nodded his head yes. His grandmother

11

smiled and gave him another big kiss, then shooed him back into the living room to relax.

"Put your feet up, buddy," Mr. Alberti shouted above the din. The crowd had moved inside. People sprawled on couches, tables and even the floor, still talking incredibly loudly.

"But I'm not tired, Dad," Paul protested. "I just took a nap in the car."

Paul stared out the window. It was still sunny and bright.

"It'll be a while before we eat," he said. "Can't I go exploring?"

Mr. Alberti frowned, but Paul could tell he was still in a good mood.

"Well, I suppose," Mr. Alberti said. "As long as you're careful. And as long as you come home in time for dinner."

"I promise," Paul called over his shoulder.

"Don't go too far," Mr. Alberti yelled over the dozen other voices that all chattered at once. "It's easy to get lost around here."

But Paul was already out the door.

# Chapter Three

Paul enjoyed nothing more than exploring something new.

Sometimes, if his friends really liked a movie — like, say, "Dinosaur Island" or "The Big Tornado" — they'd want to go see it again and again.

Paul hated that. Once he'd seen something and knew what it was like and how it was going to turn out, he was ready for something new.

Sometimes, though, his curiosity got him into a fix.

Like the time he ate some dry cat food, to find out what it tasted like. The answer, he found out, is that it tastes just like dirt.

Or the time he walked around with his eyes closed, to see what it would be like to be blind, and he fell down the stairs. His mom had to take him to the emergency room, where the doctor put seven stitches in his knee.

Still, Paul remained as curious as ever. Now, he was really curious about Pinzolo.

The first thing he noticed, as he walked along, was how old everything was. Especially compared to Chicago, where everything was new and bright and big and flashy.

In Pinzolo, most of the buildings and houses were made of stone. They were only one or two stories tall. Sometimes, they were painted a faded yellow or brown. Mostly, though, they were left their natural gray.

Paul walked over to what looked like an apartment building and touched the wall. It was cold and damp, like what a dungeon must have felt like, back in the Dark Ages. Creepy.

Everything was old, like in one of those old black-and-white *Frankenstein* movies. But something else struck Paul as curious about Pinzolo. Everything was also *deserted*. Like a ghost town.

Paul had walked around for a good ten minutes and hadn't seen a soul.

All of the stores were closed. The butcher shop, the boot store, the magazine-and-candy stand — all locked up and dark.

Paul looked at his watch. It was two o'clock in the afternoon. Where *was* everybody?

Then he remembered something his dad had told him. In Italy, everybody takes *three hours* for a lunch break. The workers all go home and eat a huge lunch and rest and spend time with their families.

*That's* why the streets were empty and the stores were all closed.

Boring!

Since there was nothing going on in the town, Paul looked up at the mountains that surrounded it. Pinzolo was at the bottom of a valley. Wherever you looked, you could see the huge, tree-covered mountain ranges looming in the distance.

The mountains were so gigantic that they made Paul feel like an ant, or like a speck of lint under a bed. They made the Sears Tower in Chicago look the size of a stack of quarters.

He decided he had to check these mountains out. Up close.

Paul remembered his dad's warning to be careful. But there was *nothing* to do in town. Zero.

What could it hurt to poke around the bottom of one little mountain?

Well, OK, one *big* mountain. But it wasn't like he was going to try and climb all the way to the top on his first day.

Somewhere in the back of Paul's head, a voice of reason whispered.

"You'll see those mountains soon enough, with your dad," it said. "Why do you have to go right now, on your first day here?"

Paul ignored it.

A few minutes later, he was hiking along a dirt road. He headed straight for what looked like the closest mountain.

And he'd left Pinzolo far behind.

# Chapter Four

After a few minutes of hiking, Paul came to a rickety old bridge.

His eyes lit up. This was exactly what he was looking for. Adventure! You'd never find an old bridge like this in Chicago. Some safety inspector would come and shut it down in a minute.

Paul pulled his plastic camera out of his pocket and snapped a picture. He kept a scrapbook of photos of odd places he'd been.

The bridge hung from a pair of cables. It ran across what used to be a decent-sized river.

At least, that's what Paul figured. Now the river was just a rock-filled gorge, with a tiny trickle of a stream running through it, as if someone had turned down the faucet.

Paul patted his belly for luck. Slowly, he began to make his way across the bridge. It wobbled and bounced, but the boards were solid.

He kept going.

He began to imagine what he would have to do if the flimsy thing collapsed. Probably grab hold of one of the cables, he thought, then swing to the opposite side, and climb to safety.

Then he remembered how hard it was to climb the rope in gym class. And that was with a mat underneath!

He gritted his teeth and kept going.

Soon enough, Paul was on the other side of the bridge. He couldn't help feeling a little disappointed.

Not that he wanted to fall into a gorge, of course. But he wouldn't have minded, say, a broken board. A *little* adventure.

Ahead of him, a narrow path wound its way into the foothills. Paul began to hike in that direction.

Soon, he was surrounded by trees. The mountains around Pinzolo were all very woodsy. There were also lots of rocks, most of them mossy and green.

The path was not a concrete sidewalk, like Paul had seen at some state parks in the United States.

This path was dirt. Old, gnarly tree roots crisscrossed it.

Parts of the path were very steep. Paul had trouble keeping his footing. But he kept going.

Finally, the path started to flatten out. Paul was glad. He wasn't exactly in the best shape, since he did like to eat so much. He couldn't wait to plop down on one of the mossy rocks and take a breather.

Between puffs and wheezes, he noticed the mushrooms.

They grew all along the side of the path, huge and brown, some of them as big as soup bowls. Paul remembered that, sometimes, Uncle Freddy sent dried-out mushrooms to Chicago. Paul's mom cooked them in stew. They were delicious.

Paul's stomach started to grumble, just from thinking about his mom's stew.

Then he came up with a brilliant plan. If he picked some fresh mushrooms and brought them back to his grandmother, she could cook them for dinner.

On his very first day in Pinzolo, he would be the hero of the feast!

There was only one problem. He didn't have

anything to put the mushrooms in.

He sat on his rock for a minute, thinking. Then he started getting hot. The sun was beating down on him from between the trees.

Suddenly, the solution hit him.

He slipped off his baggy button-down shirt and tied the ends together to create a bag. He still had on a white T-shirt.

He dropped to his hands and knees and began crawling around in the dirt and grass, looking for the fattest mushrooms.

He enjoyed himself thoroughly!

He spotted one giant mushroom growing behind a tree. He discovered another clump on a rock. Soon enough, his makeshift bag bulged with goodies.

He was enjoying himself too much to stop. He couldn't believe it. Here he was, picking mushrooms in the Italian Alps!

It wouldn't sound like much fun to his friends back in Chicago. They'd probably never seen a wild mushroom before. It wouldn't have sounded like much fun to *Paul* if someone else had told him about it.

But it was terrific. Spectacular.

A few feet ahead, he noticed the plumpest mushroom yet. He crawled to it like a hungry dog.

Just before he snatched his prize, he heard the ground crunch behind him. He felt a hot blast of breath on the back of his neck.

He whirled around.

And started to scream!

# Chapter Five

The cow stared back at Paul, calmly chewing on a mouthful of grass.

Paul turned bright red and scrambled to his feet. His heart was still beating fast.

The *last* thing he'd expected to see when he turned around was a big, ugly cow face staring at him.

"You scared me!" Paul said angrily, shaking his finger in the cow's face.

He didn't shake his finger too closely at the cow, though. He had never met a live cow before, and he wasn't sure whether they liked to bite kids.

The cow went back to munching patches of grass near the path. Paul watched her eat.

Cows are really dumb-looking, he thought.

He was still embarrassed about having screamed so loudly, but it didn't look as if anyone else was around. And the cow certainly didn't care.

"Where the heck did you come from?" Paul asked the cow. "What, are you lost?"

Then he really felt dumb. I am in the middle of the woods, he thought. Alone. Talking to a cow.

Lucky none of the kids from school could see him now!

The cow kept on grazing. She was brown, with big, sad eyes. Flies crawled all over her droopy eyes and wet nose. But she didn't seem to notice.

After a minute, Paul reached over carefully and patted her on the side. The cow ignored him. Her fur was matted and kind of rough.

"What should I call you? Bessie?" Paul asked. "Oh, wait, you're Italian. How about Sofia?"

The cow lifted her head and continued down the path.

"Hey, where are you going?" Paul called.

He decided to follow her. Cows move pretty slowly, so it wasn't hard to keep up.

The path curved. As they rounded the bend, the trees gave way to a large, grassy field. Dozens of other cows milled about, chewing grass or swatting flies with their tails.

Sofia slowly ambled over to her friends.

Paul looked around, but there didn't seem to be anyone tending the cows. He wondered what you would call someone who sat around and watched cows all day. A cow-herd?

He plucked a handful of grass and walked over to the nearest cow. This one was black. When she saw Paul, she looked up and stopped chewing.

Paul held out the grass with his palm open. The cow, without even sniffing to make sure it was good, leaned forward and swallowed the offering with a wet, slimy slurp! Then she went back to chewing at the ground.

"Gross!" Paul yelled. "Oh, man, why don't you show some manners?"

His hand was coated with cow spit.

Spying a fallen tree at the edge of the field, Paul sat down and furiously wiped his hand on a dry patch of grass. He had never been so disgusted in his entire life.

As he dried his hand on his shorts, Paul felt something fuzzy brush his shoulder.

Another stupid cow, he thought. But, glancing

back, he didn't see a cow.

He saw a hand. A hand covered with thick, brown fur.

A hand that wasn't human!

# Chapter Six

"Aaaaaaaaaaaaah!"

The cows glanced up as Paul tore through the field. Then they returned to their never-ending meal.

Paul found the path and kept on running. Even when his big feet stumbled over a tree root and he fell and skinned his knee, he got right back up and kept on running.

Even when the rickety-rackety bridge felt like it was going to collapse under his pounding legs, he kept on running.

Even when the people walking around in the streets of Pinzolo stopped and stared at the muddy, shirtless, crazy-looking stranger, he kept on running.

Paul did not stop running until he reached his grandmother's house. By then, he was too out of breath to explain what happened.

His undershirt was ripped and dirty. He had

skinned his knee. Twigs poked out of his hair. Yet, somehow, he had never dropped his shirt-bag full of mushrooms.

He handed the mushrooms to his grandmother.

"I . . . " he puffed, "picked . . . these . . . for . . . you."

His grandmother looked confused.

"Never mind that," Mr. Alberti cried. "What happened to you, buddy? Did somebody hurt you?"

"Mountains," Paul gasped. "Mushrooms . . . Monster!"

He stood there gasping frantically for air, his chest heaving, his mouth open.

"Monster?" Mr. Alberti repeated. "Come on. Sit down. Let's take it from the top."

All the other relatives had gone home to change for dinner, so Paul's grandmother and his dad were the only ones around. Paul was glad not to have had such a huge audience for this particular scene.

He sat down in the kitchen and, while his grandmother made him some hot tea, he told the whole story of the path and the mushrooms and the cows.

Mr. Alberti translated the tale into Italian for Paul's grandmother. Paul could tell he was adding things like, "I *told* him not to go too far!"

Finally, Paul got to the part about the hand.

"I swear, Dad, it wasn't human," he insisted. "It was covered with thick, black fur! It tried to grab me, but I was too fast. My T-shirt got ripped, though."

Paul paused and pushed his glasses back up his nose. He waited to hear how brave he'd been. How he was such a great adventurer.

Instead, his dad turned red and let out a huge belly laugh!

"What's so funny?" Paul howled.

Mr. Alberti told Paul's grandmother something in Italian. Then *she* started cracking up, too.

"La Barba!" she cried, holding her sides as if they would burst.

"What barber?" Paul asked. "What are you guys talking about?" He was starting to get a little steamed.

Mr. Alberti wiped tears from his eyes. That's how hard he was laughing.

28

"La Barba is the old man who takes care of the cows," Mr. Alberti finally explained. "His real name is Italo. I remember him from when *I* was a kid, so that's how old he must be. Those were his cows you were playing with. He probably wanted to find out what you were up to."

"But the *fur*," Paul protested. "I saw it with my own eyes!"

Mr. Alberti chuckled and patted his son on the back.

"That's the funny thing about old Italo," he said. "Even when I was a kid, he was the *hairiest* guy we'd ever seen. I mean head to toe! He used to scare the younger kids. That's why we called him 'La Barba.' It means 'beard' in Italian."

Paul felt himself blush. He'd been humiliated by an old coot who needed a shave! Well, he told himself, at least my dad got such a kick out of the story that he forgot to punish me for wandering off in the first place.

Still, he vowed never to tell anyone else what had happened.

After all, he didn't want people here to get the wrong idea, and think he was just another silly American.

# Chapter Seven

"So then he said, 'A monster grabbed me!' "

Everyone at the crowded dinner table howled with laughter as Mr. Alberti told the story of Paul's misadventure. In Italian, of course. But Paul didn't have much trouble figuring it out.

He managed to ignore most of the teasing. Mostly because he concentrated on something much more important.

Food!

Paul's grandmother had put together a Feast with a capital F. Paul was used to his dad saying, "We're having spaghetti for dinner tonight." And that would be all.

In Italy, spaghetti was only one course in the meal. After that came meat and vegetables and salad and cheese and fruit and dessert and, at the very end, strong Italian coffee served in tiny cups.

Paul skipped the coffee, but he had just about everything else — and massive amounts of it.

He also enjoyed the meal because he finally got to meet his cousin Anthony, Uncle Freddy's and Aunt Nat's son.

Anthony was Paul's age, and he seemed *tough*.

He was short and tan and wiry, with dark, mischievous eyes. He'd been at work earlier, painting houses, and his hands and arms were still freckled with white paint. Paul had never worked a job where he got his hands dirty. Once he'd had a paper route, but that was it.

Even better than meeting someone his own age, Paul thought, was meeting someone who spoke English. Anthony had taken English in school as a second language. He had an accent, of course. But he didn't have any trouble making himself understood.

The first thing he said to Paul was, "So. You like Chicago?"

"I like it OK," Paul replied. "But so far, I like it better here."

He wasn't trying to be polite. He really meant it.

To his surprise, a scowl crossed Anthony's face.

"Pinzolo?" he asked. "You like Pinzolo better than Chicago? What about all the big buildings in Chicago?"

"They're all right," he shrugged. "But you guys have these mountains."

Anthony snorted.

"Yes, the mountains are nice. But they were always here. Your Chicago buildings, they were made by humans."

Paul could tell his cousin was a real hot-head. He liked him immediately. Before they could continue the argument, though, yet another dinner course was served.

Mr. Alberti was just winding up his long, loud and entertaining account of Paul's run-in with La Barba. After he finished, Paul's grandmother said something in Italian. Mr. Alberti turned to Paul with a grin.

"Your Nonna wants to know if you've ever heard the legend of the Orco."

Anthony rolled his eyes from the other side of

the table.

"Don't believe these stories," he said. "They are only to scare little girls and boys." When he said "little," it sounded like "lee-tell."

"What's the Orco?" Paul asked.

Mr. Alberti smiled and translated Paul's question into Italian. The table erupted with voices — all talking at once, all talking very loud, and all talking to Paul about the Orco.

Mr. Alberti and Anthony attempted to translate.

"The Orco is a story they tell around here," Mr. Alberti began. "He's sort of like — hmm, what would you call it in English? A troll. An ugly troll that lives up in the mountains. He has great powers in the mountains, so he can find you wherever you go."

Cousin Sergio rubbed his curly hair and shouted something at Paul.

"Sergio says the Orco is hairy, like Italo," Mr. Alberti explained.

Uncle Freddy started yelling and waving his arms wildly. At first, Paul thought he might be having a fit.

"My dad says Orco has seven arms and seven legs," Anthony muttered, obviously not impressed. "But I tell you, don't believe their stories."

Aunt Nat shook her head.

"Your aunt disagrees with your uncle," Mr. Alberti translated. "She says the Orco looks just like a regular man. The only way you can tell he's the Orco is by checking his feet."

"His feet?" Paul asked.

"He has chicken's feet," Mr. Alberti explained. Paul laughed.

"See," Anthony cried. "I told you. It's silly."

"The Orco eats people," Mr. Alberti continued.

Sergio interrupted and pointed at Paul and Anthony.

"Oh, I'm sorry, I got it wrong," Mr. Alberti said, guffawing loudly. "He only eats *children*."

Paul looked at Anthony and rolled his eyes.

"Ooooh!" he said sarcastically, pretending to be afraid. Anthony giggled.

Paul's grandmother took over the story-telling. She removed her gold wedding band and held it up for everybody to see.

"Oh, this is the most important part to remember," Mr. Alberti warned. "If you ever run into the Orco, the only way to get rid of him is by throwing your wedding ring at him. The ring is a symbol of love and goodness, so the Orco will run away."

Paul flashed his dad a thumb's up sign.

"Got it," he said. "Now I'll know exactly what to do if I get into trouble."

Mr. Alberti laughed.

Anthony began explaining how, in Pinzolo, grown-ups treated kids like they were really stupid.

"I bet in Chicago, they show kids a lee-tell more respect," he grumbled.

Everyone else at the table continued talking and laughing and eating and drinking. Even though Paul had made a big show of joking around and acting brave, he couldn't help thinking about all of those Orco stories.

He didn't believe the stories, but still he tried to picture what the Orco would look like. Hairy. Ugly. With a man's body and chicken's feet.

Or even worse, with seven arms and seven

legs.

Seven hands. One to grab your left arm. One to grab your right arm.

One to grab your left leg. One to grab your right leg.

One to cover your mouth, so you couldn't scream.

And two left over to slowly wrap around your throat.

# Chapter Eight

The next morning, Paul and his dad woke up before eight. Because of the time change, it felt like three in the afternoon to them.

"It's jet lag," Mr. Alberti explained. "It takes a couple of days to get used to."

Breakfast in Italy was nowhere near as elaborate as dinner. Basically, it was some crusty rolls and a big bowl of cafe latte, which is a little bit of Italian coffee and *lots* of hot milk.

Paul never drank coffee in Chicago. But his grandmother, like all grandmothers, knew exactly what he wanted. She filled his cafe latte with lots of extra sugar. It tasted great.

After breakfast, Mr. Alberti pushed away from the table and wiped his mouth.

"We'd better give your mother a call," he said.

Paul could barely hear his mother on the

phone. She sounded very far away. She was at a hotel in Pittsburgh.

"Are you having fun?" she asked.

"Uh-huh," Paul said. "I just drank a big bowl of coffee for breakfast."

Paul's mom laughed.

"I heard you ran into the Orco already," she said.

Paul felt his face redden. His dad had talked to his mom first and said a few things in Italian. He must have told her all about the whole meeting with La Barba.

"I wasn't scared," Paul lied. "I knew it was that hairy old coot."

Paul's mom could always tell when he was lying. It never failed.

"Now Paul, I know how they like to tease over there," she said. "And I know what an imagination you have. But don't go believing every story they tell you. They're just tall tales."

"I know!" Paul whined. "I'm not a baby, you know."

"Hey, take it easy," his mom said. "I know you

don't believe it. Just make sure you're careful, OK?"

"I will," Paul said.

"And promise you won't go wandering off again without your father."

Paul mumbled something into the phone. He didn't really say *anything*. But he hoped it sounded enough like "I promise" to fool his mom.

It didn't. She knew every trick.

"Paul," she ordered, more sternly. "Promise."

"All right, all right," Paul sighed. "I promise not to go off by myself and do anything stupid."

Paul's dad and his grandmother were sitting on the couch, looking through an old photo album. They didn't notice that one of Paul's hands had disappeared up into his baggy shirt sleeve.

Or that, just as he made his promise, two of his fingers happened to be crossed.

# Chapter Nine

Since they were both still suffering from jetlag, Paul and his dad decided to put off any major sightseeing for a couple of days. The trips would be more fun if they were well rested.

"We need to start visiting relatives, anyway," Mr. Alberti said.

Paul groaned. It seemed as if *everyone* in Pinzolo was related to them somehow.

"Now, come on, buddy," Mr. Alberti said. "Aren't you interested in learning about your ancestors and finding out about your roots? It'll be like history class."

Paul kept his mouth clamped shut. He *hated* history class. His last history teacher, Mrs. Ludholz, had made them memorize the name of every single president. In order. Even Millard Fillmore!

For a moment, Mr. Alberti watched his son

squirm with unhappiness. Then the corners of his mouth started to turn upward. Finally, unable to contain himself any longer, he burst out into a long, loud laugh.

"Or," he said, catching his breath, "I suppose you could let Anthony show you around town."

Paul sighed with relief. His sore cheeks couldn't have stood another whole day of being pinched.

Twenty minutes later, Paul and Anthony were running down the front steps of their grandmother's house. Cries of "Be careful!" — in both Italian and English — echoed down the street after them.

It was still early, about 10:30 in the morning. The town was completely different from the first time Paul had seen it.

The streets were packed with people. All the shops were open. An outdoor market, teeming with people, took up several blocks. Vendors sold everything from live rabbits to fancy clothes to fresh tomatoes.

"The market comes every Wednesday," Anthony explained. "They travel to all of the towns in the valley."

Paul spotted a man selling toys and dashed over to the booth. He picked up a cool robot with seven different guns and a space chain saw.

"Sweet!" he cried. "I've never seen one of these before."

Anthony yawned.

"They're OK," he said. Then he lowered his voice, even though the vendor probably didn't speak English. "But the same people come here every week. They're nothing special. Nothing, I bet, compared to the shopping malls they have in Chicago."

Paul shrugged and put down the robot. He didn't have any money to buy it with, anyway.

"Well, malls are different, that's all, and ... "

"Tell me about America," Anthony interrupted, as they continued walking through the market. "There's nothing I want more than to travel to your country."

"Well, it's not bad," Paul offered. "The city is pretty crowded. And noisy. There are lots of cars. No mountains. It's really much better here."

Anthony looked at Paul as if he had just declared, "I am a giant, walking cheese." He raised his eyebrows and dropped his jaw. His entire face said, quite clearly, "YOU'RE CRAZY!"

"What are you talking about?" he cried. "Nothing exciting ever happens in Pinzolo. If someone's chicken lays an egg, the whole town knows. It's big news for weeks! Now in Chicago . . . "

Before Anthony could continue, a voice called out his name. A woman's voice. A very *old* voice.

The cousins turned around, and Paul found himself facing one of the oldest ladies he'd ever seen. She was hunched over, leaning on a wooden walking stick that someone had carved from a tree branch. The handle had been turned into a snarling monster's face.

How appropriate, Paul thought — and immediately felt like a jerk.

But the lady *was* creepy looking. Her face was creased and crumpled, like a dried-up apple. She had a little white mustache, and whiskers on her chin, too. And the craziest eyes!

"Ciao, Maria," Anthony called out.

The lady ignored him and mumbled something in Italian. Then — verrrry slowly — she pointed a knobby, bony finger at Paul.

Anthony answered her in Italian. Paul had no idea what they were talking about.

Suddenly, the lady's wrinkled face broke out into a hundred more wrinkles. Paul thought she might be smiling.

"Paulo!" she cried. And — verrry slowwwly — she hobbled toward Paul.

"She's a distant cousin," Anthony whispered. "Just say ciao."

"Ci-ciao," Paul stuttered meekly. He flashed Maria a lame wave. Her expression didn't change at all. She continued to hobble his way.

"You have to talk *louder*," Anthony whispered. "She's practically deaf."

"CIAO!" Paul shouted.

Several shoppers turned to look at the obnoxious American shouting "Ciao!" in the middle of the market. Even Maria seemed a little startled. But she grinned and addressed Paul in Italian.

Paul nodded politely and smiled back.

"What did she just say to me?" he whispered out of the corner of his mouth.

Maria was much closer now. And slowwwly leaning toward Paul. Her wrinkled lips parted slightly, revealing two lonely, rotten teeth.

Paul shrank back as she approached.

Anthony gave him a gentle shove forward.

"Go on," he whispered. "She said she wants a *kiss.*"

# **Chapter Ten**

"Yuck!" Paul said under his breath.

For the next five minutes, he couldn't stop wiping off his cheeks. *Both* his cheeks. They were in Italy, after all, and that was the way you got kissed. A double whammy.

For the next *ten* minutes, Anthony wouldn't stop snickering.

"You should have seen the look on your head," he laughed.

"Face!" Paul snapped.

"That's what I said," Anthony protested.

Paul didn't bother to insist.

The boys browsed through the market stalls and shops, but soon tired of it. Mostly because neither one of them had any money.

"I've got an idea," Anthony said. "I'll show

47

you the graveyard."

"Um, sure. That sounds cool," Paul lied.

He did not like graveyards. They were the one thing he *wasn't* curious about. But he didn't want his tough Italian cousin to think he was a chicken.

The graveyard sat at the edge of town. It was surrounded by a stone wall, too high to peek over. The only way to get in was through a rusty iron gate.

The boys pushed through and stepped inside.

The first thing Paul noticed was how *big* all the graves were. It seemed as if each dead person had his own life-sized statue next to his grave. There were crying angels and praying saints, usually staring into the heavens. Other graves just had giant, carved stones. Creepy, yellowed photographs of the dead person were usually attached to the stones under a glass cover.

"It'd be easy to get lost in here," Paul murmured. He heard his voice tremble. He hoped Anthony didn't notice.

"You're not scared, are you?" Anthony asked, giving his cousin a playful poke in the ribs.

"No!" Paul snapped. He tried to put Anthony

in a wrestling hold, but he was too slow.

"You'll never catch me," Anthony laughed, dashing behind a musty crypt.

Paul sprinted after him. Even as he chased his cousin, it occurred to him that there was a dead body inside that very crypt. Maybe a whole family of dead people.

He spotted Anthony at the end of a long row of graves and began racing toward him. Anthony tried to escape, but Paul's legs were longer.

Just as Paul reached to grab Anthony by the belt, the boys raced around the corner of another crypt.

And stopped dead in their tracks.

Blocking their path was the ugliest, hairiest creature Paul had ever seen!

# Chapter Eleven

"Ciao, Italo!" Anthony called out, struggling to catch his breath.

Paul blinked in the bright sunlight. He realized he was face to face with the famous La Barba. The famous and *very hairy* La Barba.

Paul could tell that La Barba was old from the wrinkles on his face. But his hair was still as black as a young man's.

And what hair! La Barba had a long, thick beard that touched his belly. The hair on his head was a shaggy mop that fell past his shoulders. His arms, his legs, and even his hands were covered with a black fuzz so thick it looked like fur. It was gross!

Paul decided then and there that if *he* ever got that hairy, he would never go around wearing only shorts and a T-shirt.

Anthony began chatting with Italo. Just like Maria, La Barba soon pointed a hairy finger at Paul and muttered something in Italian.

Oh, no! Paul thought. If *he* wants to kiss me, I'll scream!

But La Barba didn't make any sudden moves. Anthony looked confused, though. He asked Italo a question.

Italo stared at Paul, long and hard. His beady eyes peered out from the tangle of hair that surrounded them like a forest. Then he turned to Anthony and shook his head.

After they said their "ciaos" and Italo shuffled away, Paul turned to Anthony to crack a joke. But he stopped before he even started.

Anthony was as white as a blank sheet of paper.

"C-come on," Anthony stuttered. His voice, normally loud and firm, sounded frightened. "Let's get out of here."

"What's the matter?" Paul asked. Anthony didn't respond.

They left the graveyard and walked in silence

for several minutes. Then, abruptly, Anthony stopped in front of an ice cream shop. A family sat at an outdoor table, laughing and sharing their treats. The youngest girl had chocolate sauce all over her face.

Anthony turned to Paul and grabbed his arm.

"I asked Italo if he remembered you from the other day," he said softly.

"So what?" Paul asked. "He didn't seem mad at me. And why should he be? I didn't hurt any of his cows."

"That's the thing," Anthony replied, his grip on Paul's arm growing tighter. "He said he's never seen you before in his life. He wasn't there the other day. *That wasn't his hand.*"

# Chapter Twelve

"So what did you boys do today?" Mr. Alberti asked when they sat down to dinner that night.

Paul and Anthony had agreed not to say anything about the meeting with Italo in the graveyard. Just to make sure Paul remembered, Anthony gave his cousin a sharp kick under the table.

"Ow!" Paul cried.

"What's the matter?" Mr. Alberti asked.

"Um, nothing," Paul stammered. "I, uh, just stubbed my toe. On the table leg. I'm OK."

Mr. Alberti stroked his mustache curiously.

"Right," he said finally, but he did not sound convinced. He stared for a long time at Paul, then at Anthony.

Before Mr. Alberti could say anything else, Paul's grandmother brought out an enormous, steaming bowl of gnocchi. That's pronounced knee-yaw-KEY. They're Italian potato dumplings served with spaghetti sauce.

Paul had to struggle to keep himself from drooling like a wild beast. He found them *delicious.* Everybody dug in.

Two hours and five courses later, Paul and Anthony asked to be excused from the table.

"Have you been upstairs yet?" Anthony asked. Paul shook his head.

As usual, Paul had eaten too much for his own good. He felt too bloated even to speak, let alone climb stairs. Somehow he managed to follow Anthony up two whole flights.

At the top of the stairs, a doorway opened onto the flat roof of Paul's grandmother's house. A couple of folding chairs were set up there. The boys sat down.

The sun was starting to set, lighting the mountains from behind with a pink glow. It didn't seem possible, but the mountains looked even more impressive than usual.

"Wow," Paul exclaimed, adjusting his chair on

the roof. "What a view."

Anthony shrugged.

"I just like it up here because it's breezy," he said. "Now your Sears Tower in Chicago - *that* must have a magnificent view."

Paul slapped his forehead.

"Sure!" he said. "It's a magnificent view of a dirty old city! It's nothing like these mountains. I can't understand you."

"OK, OK," Anthony interrupted. "We will not agree for now."

Then he lowered his voice.

"I think you know what we really need to talk about," he said.

Paul nodded. "By the way," he added, rubbing his sore ankle, "you didn't have to kick me. I wasn't going to say anything."

"I was just being careful," Anthony shot back with a grin.

"Well, you didn't have to kick me *so hard*," Paul snapped. "So, what do you think grabbed me out there?"

He continued, nodding his head toward the

mountains.

"You think it could've been the . . . "

"There is no Orco!" Anthony barked.

He sounded like he was trying to convince himself as much as Paul.

"They've been telling me Orco stories since I was old enough to listen. And that's all they are. Stories! I can't believe you fall for that stuff."

He paused for a moment and began picking at one of the scabs on his arm. He had lots of scabs and cuts and bruises. Paul thought that made his cousin look even tougher.

Finally, Anthony added, "You're just like a little baby!"

Paul jumped up from his chair.

"I'm no baby!" he almost shouted. Remembering they were trying to keep a secret, he lowered his voice. "I want to find out what grabbed me just as much as you do. If you're so tough . . . "

He paused. He hoped he wouldn't regret what he was about to say. He plunged ahead anyway.

"If you're so tough," he said, "let's go back out there."

Anthony stared at Paul for a split second, then spat out, "Fine! It's probably a wild duck's chase anyway."

"It's *goose* chase," Paul corrected. There was a twinge of meanness in his voice.

"That's what I said!" Anthony snapped.

The cousins stared at each other in silence. Then, both at once, they laughed nervously.

"Let's not fight," Anthony said.

"OK," Paul agreed. They shook hands. "Friends."

But Paul realized that neither one of them would back down. The sun was almost gone behind the mountains now. They did not look as inviting as they had before. A cold breeze blew across the roof.

Paul shivered. Part of him didn't really believe in any old Orco. Part of him couldn't wait to go back and explore anyway.

But another part of him — the part that remembered that furry hand and its iron grip — was scared. He didn't say that out loud, though.

All he said was: "Don't worry, buddy. What could happen to *two* of us?"

# Chapter Thirteen

Over the next couple of days, Paul and his dad went sightseeing.

They took a cable car to the top of the highest mountain, and drank hot chocolate in the refuge at the summit. They borrowed Uncle Freddy's car and drove to a nearby lake. It was too cold to swim, but they dunked their feet and ate at a fancy restaurant on the water. Paul snapped lots of pictures with his plastic camera.

At the end of the week, Mr. Alberti decided to get all of his visiting out of the way in one swoop.

He invited everyone he knew — cousins, in-laws, friends, practically all of Pinzolo — to get to-gether for a huge picnic in the town park. Uncle Freddy started a fire and cooked polenta. That's pro-nounced poo-LEN-tuh, and it's a sticky yellow mush made out of cornmeal. It tastes better than it sounds, especially covered with cheese or stew. Uncle Freddy cooked the polenta over an open fire in a giant copper kettle, stirring it with a wooden ladle.

After lunch, Paul and Anthony got permission to go for a hike by themselves.

"We promise to stay on the trails," Paul said.

"And?" asked Mr. Alberti.

"We promise not to be too late."

"And?"

"Um..." Paul scratched his head. "I don't know. What?"

"Do you promise not to have any fun?" Mr. Alberti asked with a straight face.

Paul and his dad both cracked up.

"No," Mr. Alberti continued. "I want you to have fun. The only thing I want *more* is for you to be careful."

"I will, Dad," Paul insisted. "Really."

He and Anthony set off. They followed the same route Paul had taken on his first day in Pinzolo. All the way through town. Over the rickety-rackety bridge. And finally down the windy trail.

"See those painted rocks?" Anthony pointed to a rock by the side of the trail. Someone had painted a red blotch in the center of it. There were rocks like this every twenty feet or so. "That's so you can follow the trail and not get lost."

As they rounded a bend and headed toward the cow pasture, Anthony turned and pointed to a steep, overgrown incline.

"This way," he instructed.

The route Anthony wanted to take led right into the thick of the woods. It was definitely *not* the path.

"Why do you want to go that way?" Paul asked. "Whatever it was that grabbed me, it grabbed me over by the cows."

"Sure, but nothing's going to be there *today*," Anthony explained wearily. "It's Sunday. Italo's whole family comes up to his field on Sunday for a picnic. All of his kids and grandkids will be there, running around and scaring all the cows. We'll never see anything with all those people around."

"OK," Paul said. "You're the native guide."

As a native guide, Anthony was more used to

walking than Paul. Especially uphill. He was also better at dodging roots. And tree branches. And spider webs.

Paul stumbled twice. He scraped his cheek on a pointy branch and got a mouthful of cobweb. He puffed and wheezed from the climb. But the last thing he wanted to do was admit that he couldn't keep up with Anthony.

To make himself keep going, he stared again at his beat-up red sneakers. And concentrated. One foot. After another. After another.

Soon, his vivid imagination went to work and helped him pass the time.

He was a soldier. He'd been captured by the enemy and was being marched through the woods to a prison camp. They wanted to break his spirit. He'd had no food for days. They only allowed him a swallow of water from a dirty sponge. But he wouldn't give them the satisfaction of breaking. Not Paul Alberti. He'd keep walking. One foot. After another. Like a machine. An unstoppable machine.

A few minutes later, he *had* to stop. His imagination could give him only so much help.

"Anthony," he gasped, leaning against a tree, "hold on a second, I need to take a . . . "

Anthony didn't answer. Paul sucked in a deep breath and, finally, looked up from his enormous shoes. Immediately, he stopped talking.

Because there was no one to talk to. Anthony was gone.

# Chapter Fourteen

"Anthony?" Paul stammered.

His words echoed through the forest. There was no sign of his cousin. Anywhere.

"Don't panic," Paul told himself. "You're just going for a little hike in the mountains. Nothing bad has happened."

He looked around. It was dark and difficult to see. The trees were so tall they filtered out the sun. The air felt damp. Green moss covered every rock. None of the rocks had red dots.

"Don't panic," Paul repeated to himself.

Then he panicked.

"ANTHONY!" he screamed. His voice echoed through the forest.

He spun around and ran back toward the main trail. Then he got confused. Was he going in the right direction? The area was hilly. Everything looked the same.

Anthony had been breaking branches so they could find their way back. But there were lots of broken branches.

No, this way wasn't right, Paul thought.

He turned and ran the opposite way. He slipped on a tree root and landed in the dirt.

Before he could rise, a hand gripped his shoulder.

He let loose a shriek of sheer horror.

# Chapter Fifteen

Anthony cupped his other hand over Paul's mouth.

"Shut up, dummy!" he whispered fiercely.

"Anthony!" Paul cried through a mouthful of fingers.

At first he was delighted to see his cousin. Then he got mad.

"Where were you, anyway?" he asked.

"Up here," Anthony hissed. He led Paul to the top of a ridge. It was hidden by a cluster of trees and rocks.

"Look," Anthony said, pointing down the other side of the ridge.

Paul looked in the direction Anthony pointed. He saw a run-down cabin in the middle of a clearing. It was more like a shack, actually. It had a thatched roof and was made of different-sized stones that seemed loose and worn-out. Paul couldn't tell whether anyone lived in the cabin or not.

"That's why I didn't say anything," Anthony explained. "I was trying to be quiet, just in case anyone's in there."

"Sorry," Paul murmured. "You've never seen this place before?"

Anthony shook his head. "I've never even *heard* of people living up here. It's too hard to get to town."

He paused and thought and squinted a bit as he stared at the cabin.

"Well, I guess we should go down and check it out," he said.

Paul gulped. He felt his stomach twist up in knots. The polenta was like a boulder in his belly.

"All right," he heard himself say. "Let's go."

Anthony grabbed his shoulder.

"Wait," he said. He sounded embarrassed. "I, uh, want you to hold onto something."

He reached into a pocket and handed Paul something small and shiny. Paul held the object up to the light. It was his grandmother's gold wedding ring!

"You took Nonna's ring?!" Paul cried.

Anthony looked ashamed.

"I know those Orco stories are stupid," he said. "But, you know - just in case - I, uh, how do you say in English? I *borrowed* the ring this morning. She takes it off every night before she goes to bed. I snuck it out when she wasn't looking."

Paul remembered hearing his grandmother saying something about misplacing her ring.

"Borrowed it? You stole it!" he whispered fiercely. "I can't believe you just took Nonna's wedding ring. What if we lose it?"

"That's why I'm giving it to you," Anthony protested. "You have snaps on your shirt pocket, so it won't go anywhere."

"OK," Paul agreed warily. "I'll carry the ring. But we have to return it as soon as we get home."

"What do you think - that I want to sell Nonna's ring?" Anthony grumbled.

The cousins glared at each other for a moment. Then, without a word, they set off down the ridge, toward the mysterious house in the woods.

# Chapter Sixteen

"Make sure you walk quietly," Anthony warned his cousin as they made their way down the slope.

Paul tried. But he couldn't help noticing every time he made even the tiniest sound. In the silence of the mountain forest, every snapped twig sounded like a giant cracking his knuckles. Every crunched leaf sounded like a stadium full of people all munching potato chips at the exact same time.

Finally, they made it to the cabin. Everything seemed quiet. The cabin was bigger than it had looked from the top of the ridge. The only window was too high for either of them to peep through.

They crouched next to the wall, directly under the window.

"One of us must lift the other," Anthony whispered.

"Well, I'm heavier," Paul noted, patting his belly for emphasis.

"Yes," Anthony agreed, "but I'm strong." He flexed his muscles. Then he laced his hands together, palms up, to make a step.

"Well, fine," Paul said. "I'll look. I'm not afraid."

He was lying, of course. Gingerly, he stepped into Anthony's hands and felt himself being lifted toward the window.

"Mama!" Anthony whispered. "You have some big feet."

Paul couldn't believe it. Here they were, risking their lives at this creepy old cabin in the middle of nowhere, and he was still hearing about his big feet!

He didn't have much time to dwell on it, though, because soon he was gripping the window ledge.

"Got it?" Anthony grunted.

"Yes," Paul whispered.

Slowly, he pulled himself up, until he could peer into the dark, shadowy cabin. It was hard to make anything out. He teetered on Anthony's hand, trying to keep his balance.

He squinted deeper, deeper into the gloom . . . and then let go of the ledge and screamed!

# Chapter Seventeen

Anthony and Paul toppled backwards into the dirt.

"Eyes!" Paul cried. "I saw a pair of eyes, staring out at . . . "

He was interrupted by a sound coming from the window.

"Meow."

Paul and Anthony stared up at the sill. A black cat was perched there, licking itself clean.

Paul felt himself turning red. He looked at Anthony — who looked just as red as Paul felt. Dirt covered Anthony's shirt. Twigs stuck out of his hair. A small cut shone scarlet on his cheek.

He looked mad.

"You!" Anthony grunted. "You!"

Paul realized his cousin was so mad, he'd forgotten how to speak English.

"I'm sorry," Paul stammered. "I just saw those eyes and thought . . . "

"You are the biggest baby I know!" Anthony yelled. "You see a little kitty-cat and you scream like it is a bear! I can't believe you are my cousin. I tell you to be quiet and now every mouse in this forest knows we are here! And look at me! I am cut up. I am filthy. I . . . "

But now it was Paul's turn to get mad.

"Don't call *me* a baby!" he shouted. "I'm the one who climbed up there, not you! And if you had been strong enough to hold me, we wouldn't have fallen down in the first place!"

"Oh, are you saying I was scared to look in that window myself?"

"That's exactly what I'm saying!" Paul yelled.

"Well," Anthony snapped, standing up and brushing himself off, "then I guess I'd better lead the way inside."

"Fine," Paul said. He stood up and followed Anthony around to the wooden door of the cabin.

"You made so much racket, if anyone was inside, he would've come out by now," Anthony groused.

He didn't sound so tough now that he was standing in front of the door to the creepy little shack. Paul didn't feel very tough either.

"Yeah," Paul agreed. "It's *gotta* be empty."

Anthony nodded. He grabbed the door handle and pushed.

The door didn't budge.

"There's no lock," Anthony whispered. "It's just stuck." For some reason, it seemed like the right time to start whispering again.

Anthony pushed the door again, harder. It still refused to budge.

"Maybe we should just leave," Paul whispered.

Anthony glared back at him.

"You think I'm scared?" he asked.

"No," Paul protested. "It's just . . . "

Before Paul could continue, Anthony turned around and slammed into the door with his shoulder, hard.

The door gave way with loud crash and swung open, and Anthony tumbled head-first into the darkness.

# Chapter Eighteen

"Anthony!" Paul cried.

Without even thinking, he dashed in after his cousin.

Anthony lay dazed in the center of the room. Beyond that, the cabin was empty.

The old shack did not look as scary on the inside as it had from the outside. A worn-out bed occupied one corner of the room. A bare wooden table stood unevenly in the middle of the floor. A half-empty jug of wine sat on a shelf. Some old sections of pipe lay on the floor, and the corners of the room were filled with dust and cobwebs.

And that was about it.

"Are you OK?" Paul asked his cousin.

Anthony stood up angrily and brushed himself off, yet again.

"I'm fine," he snapped. But he seemed embarrassed about his fall. "This place is a dump," he added.

Paul nodded in agreement.

"You think anyone still lives here?" he asked.

"I don't know," Anthony said. "Everything's so old and dusty."

As if he wanted to emphasize the point, Paul sneezed loudly. All over Anthony.

"Sorry," he said. "I'm allergic to dust."

Anthony wiped off his face without a word. Then he dropped to his knees and peered under the bed.

"Nothing down here," he reported.

Paul turned to the shelf on the wall. Aside from the wine jug, there was a glass, a melted-down candle and a dirty kitchen knife. He picked up the knife and touched the tip. It was still sharp.

"Hey," he said. "Come look at this."

Before Anthony could respond, a horrible, high-pitched sound split the air.

Paul and Anthony both jumped about three feet into the air. Paul took a deep breath and looked toward the door.

The noise had come from the cat. Paul had never in his life heard a cat hiss that way. All of its black fur was standing on end. It stood by the open door, and seemed very scared.

Then it arched its back and screeched again.

"You think it's trying to tell us something," Paul asked.

"Yes," Anthony said. "Maybe that something's coming."

# Chapter Nineteen

The cat continued screeching - uttering a high wail so frightening it made the hair on Paul's neck stand up like the cat's.

Paul and Anthony ran to the door and peeked outside. No one was around. Everything looked the same.

But different, too. The little bit of sun that had leaked through the thick tree tops earlier had disappeared. Dark storm clouds massed overhead. The air felt suddenly cold and damp.

Paul shivered.

"Something weird is going on," Anthony said.

"I know," Paul said. "Maybe we should really split this time."

"Split?" Anthony had a confused look on his face. "What should we split?"

Before Paul could start another lesson in American slang, they felt the first rumble.

Paul had read about earthquakes in California, and that's what the rumbling felt like. The ground beneath their feet was shaking. Not enough to make trees fall down or the cabin crumble around them.

But more than enough for Paul and Anthony to feel it.

Something really *was* coming. Every time they felt a tremor, they heard a stomping sound in the distance. It sounded a lot like footsteps. The huge, thunderous footsteps of something really, *really* big.

They heard the snap of branches breaking. The noise came from the top of the ridge. The trees up that way were shaking.

Whatever it was, it was close.

Then they heard the howl. It sounded like it was part bear, part wolf, and maybe part something else.

But definitely not human at all.

# Chapter Twenty

The boys dashed back into the cabin and slammed the door.

The cat raced around inside the room, hissing wildly.

"Shut up!" Paul yelled at the cat. He turned to Anthony. They stood next to each other with their backs against the door.

"Do you think it's . . . " Paul began, his voice trembling.

"I don't know," Anthony breathed. The ground continued to shake. "We'd better block off this door."

The boys ran to the heavy wooden table and dragged it toward the door as fast as they could.

The terrible footsteps grew louder, the shaking of the ground more intense.

"All right," Anthony ordered. "Push it under the handle."

With a massive shove, they wedge the table under the door knob.

The rumbles grew more thunderous. The jug of wine rattled on the shelf with each approaching footstep. Whatever it was, it was getting closer.

"That's not going to keep anything out for long," Paul cried. He couldn't stop his voice from shaking.

"You're right," Anthony said. "The only other way out is the window."

The window. So tiny. So *high*.

It's our only hope, Paul thought. He grabbed an old, rickety chair from the corner of the room and dragged it over to the window.

The stomps were getting closer.

"You go first," Anthony said.

"No!" Paul cried. "You go. I'll hold the chair steady."

Anthony shook his head.

The stomps were getting louder. The wine jug was almost jumping off the shelf.

"You're stronger!" Paul shouted. "It'll be easier for you to get the window open."

Anthony thought for a second, then nodded.

"All right," he said. "I'll do it."

"Hurry!" Paul yelled.

Anthony climbed onto the chair. He tried the window. It wouldn't budge.

"It's stuck!" he cried.

The chair was bouncing with each thunderous footstep. Paul could hardly hold it still.

"Break it!" Paul shouted.

Anthony closed his eyes and punched the window.

"Ow!" he grunted. Blood dripped from his hand. He smashed away the rest of the glass and pulled himself through the window.

The horrible hammering of the footsteps approached. It sounded as if the next step would stomp the shack flat.

Frantically, Paul looked up. He saw Anthony's feet disappear through the window. He heard Anthony fall to the ground outside with a thud.

My turn, Paul thought. He stepped onto the

chair with one of his oversized red sneakers.

And immediately felt the old chair crack.

He tumbled to the ground. His glasses flew off and slid across the floor. The chair broke into a half-dozen pieces. Paul squinted up at the window. He could not possibly reach it now.

The stomping stopped.

Paul turned and looked at the door. The door started to shake.

Whatever it was, it was here.

# Chapter Twenty-One

As he cowered in the corner, Paul heard the sound of a massive shove against the door. The table split apart and the door crashed open. Shards of wood flew across the room.

Paul covered his face.

When he opened his eyes, a blurry shape filled the doorway. Paul had trouble making it out without his glasses. But the shape was tall and dark, with two arms and two legs. It looked as if it was covered with a thick fur.

Paul could not see well, but he could smell. The shape smelled like a wet dog. Like a zoo on a hot summer day.

Like an *animal*.

Terror shot up Paul's spine like an electric shock. There was no doubt about it: He was face to face with the Orco!

Then the Orco roared. Paul thought his eardrums would burst. Even though he was all the way on the other side of the shack, Paul felt a blast of the creature's hot, foul breath.

I'm dead, he thought. There's no escape.

Another growl came from the shape in the door.

Paul was too scared to get up. Or try to run. Or even scream.

What would be the point? They were on a mountain. In the middle of nowhere. This wasn't a movie. No superhero would fly to his rescue.

The shape started to move. It bent down to fit through the doorway, and entered the cabin. And headed slowly — but surely — for Paul.

Squinting across the cabin, Paul saw that the blurry shape had something tied around its furry waist — a belt, perhaps, or a rope. A bulging sack hung from the belt.

Paul wondered if the sack contained treasure. Or the skulls of the Orco's victims. Or both. Maybe, to an Orco, a skull *was* treasure.

Paul flattened himself against the wall.

The blurry shape did not seem to have chicken's feet, he saw. They looked more or less like human's feet. Only hairier.

The Orco lumbered forward. I'm about to die, Paul thought. This is it.

He grabbed one of the broken chair legs. At least I'll go out with a fight, he thought.

Then he remembered his grandmother's ring!

The Orco was halfway across the shack now. He seemed to be taking his time. He paused to roar even louder. Paul's ears rang like it was a fire drill.

He fumbled with the snap on his pocket. The Orco took another step forward, snarling.

Paul ripped his pocket open and grabbed the ring. The Orco took another step. Paul thought he could see something dripping from the blurry shape's mouth.

Was he drooling?

Paul gulped. He had never had a great arm for football or baseball. But he hurled that ring as hard as he could.

The ring sailed through the air like a missile, straight and true. It walloped the shape smack in the center of its hairy chest.

Then it dropped to the floor and rolled into the corner.

The Orco growled and snarled and roared.

Oh no! Paul thought. I've made him *madder*!

# Chapter Twenty-Two

Now Paul knew he was dead meat.

The Orco took another step closer. Paul was too scared to move.

Then, from in the doorway, Paul heard a scream.

"AIIIIEEEEE!"

The Orco heard it, too. He stopped in his tracks and whirled around.

Paul squinted at the doorway and made out a smaller shape. Anthony! It looked like his cousin was holding something small in his right hand. Something *glowing*.

As the Orco turned his head, Anthony hurled the object into the center of the cabin.

Paul saw that it was a tiny ball. What was Anthony doing?

Suddenly, sparks shot out of the ball. The Orco took a step back. A cloud of thick green smoke billowed out of the ball. The Orco howled and took another step backwards.

It was a smoke bomb!

Paul had bought some on the Fourth of July once. He didn't know they sold them in Italy. Or that Anthony had brought any along.

But he wasn't complaining! For some reason, the Orco was *scared*. He stumbled back to the wall and waved madly at the smoke.

This is my chance, Paul thought.

He scrambled to his feet and darted through the smoke to the door, to freedom! As he ran, he reached down and snatched his glasses off the floor.

From the midst of the smoke behind him, the Orco howled.

Anthony was waiting outside.

"Let's get out of here," he cried.

They heard the Orco thrashing around in the shack. But they never looked back. They ran up the ridge and back down to the trail, and all the way back to Pinzolo.

# Chapter Twenty-Three

"He was *huge*," Paul huffed.

"He was *ugly*," Anthony puffed.

Mr. Alberti watched the boys. He frowned and folded his arms.

"OK, you guys really have to calm down," he said. "Nothing you've said so far has made any sense. Now, Paul, just take a deep breath and start over again. At the beginning."

Paul took a deep breath and started at the beginning. He told his dad about meeting La Barba in the graveyard, about leaving the path and hiking up the side of the mountain, about finding the old shack and going inside, about the clouds, the rumbling, the Orco, the ring, the . . .

"Hold it!" Mr. Alberti cried. "Where's your grandmother's ring now?"

Paul and Anthony looked at each other and gulped.

"Well, um, like I said, Dad, I threw it at the Orco," Paul said sheepishly. "But it didn't do anything to him."

"So where is the ring *now*?" Mr. Alberti asked. His voice was low and his teeth were clenched. Two bad signs.

"Um," Paul stammered. "Well, it bounced off the Orco's chest and, uh, rolled away. My glasses fell off, so I couldn't really see where it went. But I guess it's still in the shack. We didn't really have a chance to look for it, because Anthony threw in this smoke bomb and the Orco was roaring and waving his arms around and . . . "

"Enough about the Orco!" Mr. Alberti shouted. "I don't want to hear another word from either one of you about it. There is no Orco and you know it!"

"But Uncle, we . . . " Anthony began. Paul's dad cut him off.

"I told you not to go back to that mountain, but you did," he said. "You went to play silly games, and you took your grandmother's wedding ring and lost it. And now you've made up an imaginary Orco to make it seem all right. Well it's *not* all right! Do you know how your grandmother will feel when she finds out that ring is lost? Do you?"

Paul and Anthony both stared at their shoes.

Paul had never seen his dad this angry. Not even the time Paul had been trying to use Mr. Alberti's electric razor, just to see what it would feel like, and had accidentally dropped it into the toilet.

Mr. Alberti stared at the boys a few moments, letting them writhe under his gaze.

"OK," he said finally. "Let's go."

Paul looked up. Oh no! he thought. Were they going back to Chicago? Was his father that furious?

"Where — where are we going?" Paul finally stuttered.

"To find your grandmother's ring," Mr. Alberti stated firmly. "You are taking me to the mountain."

# Chapter Twenty-Four

No amount of begging or pleading did any good. Mr. Alberti simply did not believe that they had encountered the Orco.

And so, after Anthony's cut hand had been bandaged by their grandmother, they headed back to the last place in the world Paul ever wanted to see again — the mountain.

They hiked in silence. Mr. Alberti was too angry to say much. Paul and Anthony were too scared to say anything.

They made their way along the trail and up through the mountain forest. Finally, they came to the clearing and spied the old cabin.

"Well," Mr. Alberti snorted. "At least you were telling the truth about *something*."

Paul was not really listening to his father. He

was too busy looking for the Orco.

What was that shape, there, behind the tree?

Oh. Only a bird.

Wait - there, behind Anthony, were two hands, about to grab him!

Oh. Only some branches in the wind.

"Well, come on, you two," Mr. Alberti said sharply. "We have some searching to do."

With that, he began to make his way toward the cabin. Paul and Anthony stared at each other, then reluctantly followed.

Mr. Alberti marched straight for the door. The Orco *can't* still be in there, Paul thought feverishly. Plus he only goes after kids.

Paul heard his dad say something in Italian.

Paul and Anthony rushed to the door of the cabin and peered inside. There, sitting on the edge of the bed, petting the black cat, was a man.

He looked like he was about Mr. Alberti's age. He had messy hair and a beard, and he wore shabby clothes. One of his toes poked out from a hole in his boot.

Mr. Alberti turned to Paul and Anthony. He

looked even angrier than before.

"Did you two destroy this man's house?" he asked. His voice was so low it was almost a whisper. A *very* bad sign.

Paul looked around. The chair lay smashed beneath the broken window. Pieces of table were scattered all over the floor. The whole place stank of smoke.

Paul gulped.

"I swear, Dad, it was the Orco," he began. Mr. Alberti cut him off.

"What did I tell you guys about making up stories? I don't want to hear it!" he ordered.

But the man on the bed had perked up when he heard the word Orco. He said something to Paul's dad in Italian.

"What did he say?" Paul whispered to Anthony.

"He told your dad that he's never seen the Orco before, but that he believes in it," Anthony said softly. "He told your dad that the moment he stepped in the door, he sensed something strange. Something *evil*."

The man continued talking to Mr. Alberti, who could not get a word in edgewise. Anthony listened and whispered rough translations to Paul.

"He says his name is Gianni. He lives here all by himself, with only the cat. He says he came up here because Pinzolo got too *crowded*." Anthony snorted, then added in a sarcastic tone, "Oh, yeah, it's real crowded, it . . . "

"Never mind what you think," Paul interrupted. "What else?"

Anthony glared at his cousin, but continued.

"He hunts all of his food, and picks wild fruit and mushrooms. He hates modern technology. He's going to write a book about how much he hates civilization, but right now it's all in his head."

"What about the Orco?" Paul asked.

"I'm just translating. I can't control what he talks about," Anthony snapped. "Oh, wait! He's coming back to the Orco now. He says he used to think it was all just a story, but now he believes it. He thinks the Orco used to be a man, but fell victim to a horrible curse. Now he must roam the mountain forever. He can only feast on innocent blood — either animals or children."

Anthony gulped, then continued.

"He says he finds bones sometimes, deep in the forest, of deer and wolves. He can tell it's not the work of a hunter. And he says look at all the children who wind up missing every year. The papers say they got lost or kidnapped or ran away from home."

Anthony paused again and shivered.

"He thinks it's the Orco."

Mr. Alberti tried to cut in, but Gianni ignored him and continued his speech.

"I guess he misses talking to people," Anthony muttered. "Oh, he says he thinks the Orco has always lived on the mountain. That he's almost like a part of the mountain."

Anthony paused and gulped.

"And he says that if the Orco is after you, and he wants to find you — he *will*."

# Chapter Twenty-Five

"See!" Mr. Alberti snorted after they'd left. "The only one who believes your crazy Orco stories is nuts himself!"

"Nuts?" Anthony asked, puzzled. "A person is the same as some nuts?"

No one offered to translate for him.

Paul's dad was still pretty upset. They had searched the cabin for over an hour, but they had found no sign of the ring. Gianni swore he didn't take it, and Mr. Alberti said he believed him. It was obvious Gianni did not care much about money or buying expensive things.

When they got back to Pinzolo, Mr. Alberti had to tell Paul's grandmother about the missing ring. She acted like it did not matter that much to her.

"I like you still," she told Paul over and over, patting him gently on the head.

But Paul noticed a teardrop glistening in the corner of her eye.

Uncle Freddy and Aunt Nat were more vocal. They decided, together with Paul's dad, that Paul and Anthony would forfeit their allowances every week until they paid for a new ring — *and* new furniture for Gianni's cabin.

Even worse, they decided Paul and Anthony should be separated for the rest of the visit!

"You two get into too much trouble together," Mr. Alberti said sternly. "You're lucky I'm not putting you on a plane and sending you right back to Chicago."

"But we're going to pay for the furniture and the ring," Paul protested. "Isn't that enough?"

"No," Mr. Alberti said softly. He sounded sad. "Actually, it's not nearly enough. That wedding ring had sentimental value to your grandmother. You can never replace something like that. Not ever."

Paul slunk back up to his room. His dad was right. He felt like a heel.

The next few days were horrible. Paul ate, slept, went for walks in town by himself. His grandmother never said a nasty word. But she moped around the house and did not sing and smile as she had before.

And word had gotten around Pinzolo about the ring — how Anthony and his American cousin had lost it while playing a silly Orco game in the mountains. It was a small town and news traveled fast. Wherever Paul went, he could feel people shooting him dirty looks and whispering about rotten American kids.

After a while, he started spending most of the day in his room, reading.

The family still ate lunch and dinner together at the big table in Paul's grandmother's house. There was only one difference — no Anthony. He had to stay home during meals. Afterwards, Uncle Freddy and Aunt Nat would bring him the leftovers for his supper.

One night after he had finished eating, Paul excused himself and went back to his room. He'd brought with him to Italy a thick spy novel from the grown-up section of the library. He had figured he'd be so busy having fun, the book would last him the whole summer. But now he was almost done with it.

Flopping down on his bed, he opened the novel to where he'd left off. Manly Manford, the British secret agent, was trying to defuse a bomb with one hand and beat the evil Dr. Crow in a sword fight with the other.

Before Paul could get back to the action, he noticed something odd. His bookmark had been replaced by a note!

As soon as he opened it, Paul knew the note was from Anthony. He could tell by the misspelled English words and awkward sentences. Anthony could speak English better than he could write it. He must have snuck into Paul's room while the family was eating dinner.

The note said: "PAULO — MEAT ME ON TOP OF HOWSE — TALK WE MUST — A."

Paul slipped out of his room and stood by the stairs, listening. The family was still at the dinner table, chatting loudly. Slowly, his heart pounding, Paul crept up to the roof.

Anthony was crouching in the shadows, watching the sunset.

"Hey," Paul said.

Anthony nodded. "So how has your vacation been?"

Paul rolled his eyes and sat down next to his cousin.

"This whole thing stinks," he said. "We lost Nonna's ring. Nobody believes us about the Orco. We aren't even allowed to talk."

"I know," Anthony said. "That's why we need a plan."

Paul's eyes widened. "What do you mean?"

Anthony blew back a wisp of hair that had fallen into his eyes.

"Well," he said, "the only way to make things better is to get that ring back."

"Yeah, but it's lost," Paul said glumly.

"Lost," Anthony asked, "or stolen? Did you notice a sack hanging from Orco's side?"

"Yes!" Paul exclaimed. "I remember. You think he took the ring?"

"Where else would it be?" Anthony said. "If

what Gianni said is true and Orco was once human, he might still like human things."

Paul's face fell again.

"But now we'll never get it back," he said.

"Why not?" asked Anthony. He reached into his pocket and pulled out a handful of tiny colored balls. They had fuses on the ends.

Smoke bombs.

"We know how to take care of that Orco," he said. "We can get the ring back. And if you bring your camera, we can prove once and for all that there is such a thing as the Orco."

Paul's stomach fluttered. Anthony hadn't gotten a good look at the Orco.

Of course, Paul hadn't really gotten a good look at the Orco either, without his glasses. But he'd gotten a *sense* of the Orco - and he sure didn't like it.

On the other hand, he wanted to get that ring back for his grandmother more than anything. And they had outsmarted the Orco before.

This time, they would be prepared.

And Paul's curiosity was rising again. He really wanted to get a better look at the Orco, no matter how scary it was. And a photograph! Imagine what a sensation that would cause.

His dad would have to believe him. His dad would have to *apologize*. The picture would appear in magazines and newspapers. He could write a book . . .

Then Paul thought of one small problem.

"How will we ever find the Orco again?" he asked.

Anthony nodded toward the mountains. The sun glowed pink behind them.

"We won't find him," he said. "We'll let him find us."

# Chapter Twenty-Six

The next day was Sunday. It was also a big holiday in the northern part of Italy, the feast of some saint that Paul had never heard of.

Everyone in Pinzolo celebrated by taking the ski lift to a point near the top of the tallest mountain, where there was a hotel and a restaurant. They set up tents and games and an open space for dancing.

The festival was the first time in almost a week that Paul and Anthony were allowed to be in the same place at the same time. Of course, they still weren't supposed to play together. Or even talk.

But when they were on the roof, they had made plans to slip away from the party after lunch.

They met behind a huge rock on the far side of the hotel, where no one would see them. Italian folk music blared in the distance, mingling with the voices of the partygoers.

"You ready?" Paul asked.

Anthony nodded grimly and patted his pockets.

"I've got our weapons," he replied. "Follow me."

The cousins set off down a secluded trail Anthony said he had hiked before. The trail wound away from the hotel and restaurant, up toward the white peak of the mountain.

As they walked along, the trail became icier. Soon, they were surrounded by snow.

"How much farther?" Paul wheezed. They had not walked far, but he was already out of breath.

"It's not too far," Anthony replied.

About a half-hour later, they came to a flat, snow-covered clearing. It was a lookout point, where people often stopped to take pictures of the view.

Because of the party, no one was around today. A couple of stone benches stood next to a large metal plaque that was covered with dozens of names.

"What's that?" Paul asked, nodding toward the plaque.

"Those are the names of all the people who

have died while they were hiking up here," Anthony replied matter-of-factly.

Paul gulped.

"Look over here," Anthony called. He led his cousin to the edge of the clearing. Paul got dizzy as soon as he approached. He peered over a steep drop off the side of the mountain. He could not see the bottom. But he knew it was a long way down.

"I'll wait over by the benches," he stammered, stepping away from the cliff.

Anthony laughed. But he seemed nervous, too.

"This is the spot where my friend Anita said she saw the Orco," he said.

"Really?" Paul asked. "Is that why you picked this place?"

Anthony nodded. "She was hiking with her parents and they became separated. She was sitting on that bench. Right where you're sitting."

Paul glanced down at the bench and gulped loudly.

"She saw a strange shape move in those trees over there," Anthony continued. "She started to scream. Her parents came running around up the trail.

And then the shape was gone. Just like that. We all thought she made the whole thing up."

"Now we know better," Paul muttered. "So you think he'll show up today?"

"I don't know," Anthony replied. "He's found you twice already."

The third time's the charm, Paul thought grimly, and shivered. It wasn't because he was cold.

# Chapter Twenty-Seven

Paul checked his wristwatch for the third time in five minutes. An hour had passed since they had arrived at the lookout point.

There was still no sign of the Orco.

"I don't think he's showing up," Paul said. He tried not to sound hopeful about it, but he couldn't help it.

Anthony paced back and forth near the edge of the cliff.

"We can't go back now," he cried. "Come on. Let's talk about something better. How about American cities!"

"I don't know why you're so obsessed with America, Chicago, the city!" Paul snapped. "It's way better over here."

Anthony shook his head. "You're crazy!"

*"You're* crazy!" Paul shot back. "It's so peaceful here!"

"Peaceful!" Anthony shouted. "Maybe if you're here on a three-week vacation. For me, it's boring!"

"How can it be boring?" Paul asked. "You could hike in these mountains every day."

"But there's no shopping mall," Anthony interrupted. "The only movie theater is three towns away. And you can't find a good hamburger anywhere!"

"A hamburger!" Paul cried. That was the last straw! Anthony shouldn't have started talking about food. "How can you compare a lousy old hamburger to the kind of feasts you have here?"

"Easy!" Anthony yelled. "I . . . "

Then Paul noticed something very strange. Anthony's mouth continued to move, but Paul could not hear him. All he heard was a loud rumbling. The rumbling was as loud as an eighty-person, all-drum orchestra. As loud as a jumbo jet buzzing two inches over your head.

As loud as if the Orco was coming.

"Do you think that's him?" Paul shouted. But

Anthony had turned completely white. His mouth moved, but Paul could not hear a word he was saying.

"What?" Paul cried.

Anthony pointed at something above Paul's head.

Paul whirled around and his eyes widened in terror.

"Avalanche!" he shouted.

# Chapter Twenty-Eight

If you're ever caught in an avalanche, shouting "Avalanche!" probably isn't the best idea.

First of all, everyone around you already knows it's an avalanche. Second, there's a good chance you'll end up with a mouthful of snow.

That's what happened to Paul. For about a second, he got a look at the mountain of snow hurtling down from above.

It's like an all-white tidal wave, he thought.

Then the wave hit. And it sure didn't feel like water. It felt like a truck.

Everything around Paul became white. He couldn't breathe. He felt himself flying through space. Over the edge!

Seconds later, he slammed into something solid.

Then everything was still. And silent.

Paul opened his eyes and spit the snow out of his mouth. Dazed, he sat up and shook his head.

Everything still looked completely white. He wondered if he was dead.

Then he looked up. About ten feet above his head he saw the edge of the lookout point. He had landed on a narrow ridge just below.

He glanced over his shoulder at the edge of the ridge. Below him yawned nothing but wide-open space. If he fell again, he would not get a second chance.

He moaned in pain. Every bone in his body ached. He felt as if he'd just been pelted by a hundred snowballs. He definitely didn't feel like moving.

Maybe it wasn't a full avalanche, he thought.

Then a horrible thought struck him. Where was Anthony?

"Anthony!" he cried. He crawled desperately to the edge of the ridge.

"Anthony!" he cried again. His voice echoed between the ridges and peaks.

Then he felt a hand grab his shoulder.

"Oh, Anthony," Paul said happily, whirling around. "I thought you were . . . "

Paul stopped, mid-sentence, his mouth hanging open, the words frozen in his throat.

It was not Anthony he was facing.

It was the Orco!

# Chapter Twenty-Nine

This time, Paul got a good look at the Orco. *Too* good a look. He was only inches from the Orco's face!

The Orco's face reminded Paul of pictures of cavemen you see in textbooks. A wide, high forehead set over thick eyebrows. A jutting jaw.

But, unlike a caveman, the Orco had a full set of yellow, pointy teeth.

And fur. Lots and lots of long, brown, tangly fur. On his head, on his cheeks, on his chin. All over his entire body.

Paul was close enough to see the twigs and bugs and flecks of dirt caught in the Orco's fur. He was close enough to stare into the Orco's beady, evil eyes.

Paul noticed all of these things in about two

seconds. Then he screamed.

The Orco wrapped one of his huge, hairy paws around Paul's arm and lifted him off the ground.

I'm dead, Paul thought. He tried to struggle free, but he could not break the Orco's iron grip. The long claws dug into Paul's arm.

I'm dead, he thought again.

He was eight feet off the ground, dangling like a fish on a hook, eye-to-eye with the towering Orco. A stream of drool dangled from the Orco's mouth.

The Orco began to slowly open his mouth, wide. Paul got a better look at those teeth. So yellow. So sharp. So *many*.

Suddenly, Paul heard a whistle.

Out of the corner of his eye, he saw something sail through the air and — SMACK! — nail the Orco right in the side of the head. Whatever it was exploded on impact. The Orco howled with rage.

It was a snowball.

It was Anthony!

Paul looked over to the far end of the ridge and saw his cousin, soaked from head to toe in snow, but still standing.

"Anthony! You're alive!" he shouted.

The Orco was greeting Anthony as well, but with a nasty growl. Anthony shouted back at the Orco. He was speaking in Italian, but it sounded quite rude to Paul.

The Orco roared louder. Paul's ears began ringing. He tried not to inhale the Orco's foul breath.

From the other side of the ridge, Anthony made wild gestures at the Orco with one hand and reached into his pocket with the other.

The Orco lumbered toward Anthony, still hanging on to Paul.

Anthony pulled out his secret weapon — the smoke bombs, along with a box of matches!

The Orco snarled.

"Drop my cousin, you ugly kitty!" Anthony yelled in English.

"I think you mean, 'you ugly *dog!*' " Paul called out weakly.

"That's what I said!" Anthony shouted. He sounded annoyed.

The arm from which Paul was dangling hurt badly. He *was* too heavy, he realized. If he got out of this alive, he'd have to go on a diet!

The Orco took another step closer. Anthony pulled out a match to light the smoke bomb. He struck the match against the side of the box. The match crumpled and bent in two.

With growing horror, Paul realized what was wrong.

The matches were all soaking wet from the snow. They would not light!

# Chapter Thirty

The Orco tightened his grip on Paul and took another step toward Anthony.

We're dead, Paul thought for the third time.

Then his hand brushed against his pocket, and he felt a bulky object.

The camera!

Anthony looked up at the Orco. Step by step he backed away.

But there was only so far he could go before he came to the edge of the ridge.

One more step and Anthony would sail into the void and fall to his death!

Paul managed to grab the camera with his free hand. If only he could remember how to work the flash!

The Orco took another step forward.

Paul spotted a red button on the top of the camera. FLASH. That was it!

He jabbed the button with his thumb. A flash bulb popped up from the top of the camera.

Oh, no, Paul thought. It takes a second for the flash to activate!

The Orco towered over Anthony.

Anthony cringed on his knees, covering his face.

A light on the back of the camera started to blink. The flash was ready!

"Hey, you!" Paul shouted as loudly as he could, right into the Orco's ear. The Orco turned his head to face Paul and growled horribly.

Paul pressed the flash button. The light exploded inches from the Orco's face.

The Orco howled with rage. He twisted his ugly face until it was even uglier.

He also dropped Paul to the ground. He had been blinded by the flash!

"Grab the sack!" Paul yelled. Anthony leaped to his feet and yanked at the bundle on the Orco's belt.

The Orco could not see a thing. He swiped

blindly at whatever was pulling on his belt.

Anthony was too quick, though, and managed to duck.

The Orco was off-balance. He teetered right on the edge of the cliff! He stumbled, took a step back and stumbled again, waving around his arms desperately.

Anthony clung to the sack, trying to pull it off the belt. The Orco was starting to fall backwards.

"Anthony!" Paul cried. He grabbed his cousin by the leg.

The weight of the two of them together snapped the sack from the Orco's belt. Paul and Anthony tumbled backward into the snow.

With a terrific growl, the Orco fell in the opposite direction. Right over the edge. Right into the gorge.

His howl echoed through the mountains for a full minute before dying out.

Then there was silence.

# Chapter Thirty-One

"And then," Paul huffed, "we climbed back up to the main trail."

"And then," Anthony puffed, "we ran all the way back here."

Mr. Alberti shook his head grimly.

"And you guys think this crazy story will make me forget that you two were not supposed to be playing together?"

"But we have proof!" Paul cried. He yanked the camera out of his pocket and handed it to his dad.

Mr. Alberti examined the camera for a moment and then shook his head.

"Buddy," he chuckled, "the only proof we have here is how forgetful you two can be. There's no film in this camera!"

"Oh no!" Paul shouted. "I can't believe it!"

"Wait!" Anthony interrupted. "The sack!"

It was true. They'd been in such a hurry to get back to their parents, they'd forgotten to check their prize.

"Hurry, dump it out!" Paul said.

Anthony emptied the sack on the ground — and the boys found themselves staring at a big pile of mushrooms.

"Hmm," Mr. Alberti snorted. "You guys found some pretty good ones."

Paul's heart sank. "I can't believe it. I . . . "

"Hey, wait a minute," Mr. Alberti interrupted. "I thought I saw something shiny."

He reached into the pile of mushrooms and picked up a small object. It was shiny. It was round.

It was the ring!

"All riiggght!" Paul and Anthony cried out at once.

"Well I'll . . . " Mr. Alberti began. Then words failed him.

He stopped and stared at the cousins.

"I don't know where you two found this, but

your grandmother is going to be very happy."

He stood up.

"In fact, I'm going to give it to her right now," he said. "Then I'll want the *truth*."

As he turned to leave, his stern look melted into a grin.

"In the meantime," he said, "I guess this means the ban is off. You guys are free to hang around together."

"All riiggght!" Paul and Anthony cried out for the second time.

After Mr. Alberti left, Paul looked at his cousin.

"So," he asked, "what should we tell them? They'll never believe the Orco story."

"You're right," Anthony said, shaking his head with disgust. "*Adults*. Well, we'll have to come up with something good."

"No problem," Paul replied. "We'll just think of something really boring. Adults are bound to believe that."

They looked at each other and smiled.

"Hey," Paul said, "when are you coming to

visit me in Chicago?"

"Maybe next summer," Anthony said. Then he smiled and added, "Now *that* should be an exciting vacation."

"I can't believe you!" Paul shouted.

"You are some nuts!" Anthony shouted back.

They clasped hands and grinned. And their laughter echoed through the mountains as the sun began to set.

# LET, LET, LET THE MAILMAN GIVE YOU COLD, CLAMMY *SHIVERS! SHIVERS! SHIVERS!!!*

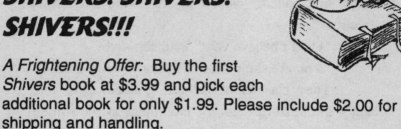

*A Frightening Offer:* Buy the first *Shivers* book at $3.99 and pick each additional book for only $1.99. Please include $2.00 for shipping and handling.

Canadian orders: Please add $1.00 per book.

___ #1 The Enchanted Attic
___ #2 A Ghastly Shade of Green
___ #3 The Awful Apple Orchard
___ #4 The Animal Rebellion
___ #5 The Locked Room
___ #6 Terror on Troll Mountain
___ #7 The Haunting House

___ #8 The Mystic's Spell
___ #9 The Ghost Writer
___ #10 The Curse of the New Kid
___ #11 Guess Who's Coming For Dinner?
___ #12 The Secret of Fern Island

I'm scared, but please send me the books checked above.

$_____ is enclosed.

Name_____

Address _____

City_____ State_____ Zip _____

**Payment only in U.S. Funds. Please no cash or C.O.D.s. Send to: Paradise Press, 8551 Sunrise Blvd. #302, Plantation, FL 33322.**